One Cow Coughs

A Counting Book for the Sick and Miserable

Story by **Christine Loomis**   Pictures by **Pat Dypold**

Ticknor & Fields Books for Young Readers   New Y

Published by

Ticknor & Fields Books for Young Readers

A Houghton Mifflin company, 215 Park Avenue South,

New York, New York 10003.

Manufactured in the United States of America

Book design by David Saylor

The text of this book is set in 28 point Avant Garde Demi

The illustrations are cut paper, reproduced in full color

HOR 10 9 8 7 6 5 4 3 2 1

Library of Congress Cataloging-in-Publication Data

Loomis, Christine.

One cow coughs : a counting book for the sick and miserable / by Christine Loomis; illustrated by Pat Dypold.   p. cm.

Summary: Animals count from one to ten and back down again as they show symptoms of illness and then, after taking care of themselves, feel better again.   ISBN 0-395-67899-4

(1. Counting. 2. Sick—Fiction. 3. Animals—Fiction. 4. Medicine—Fiction. 5. Stories in rhyme.) I. Dypold, Pat, ill. II. Title.

PZ8.3.L8619On 1994   (E)—dc20   93-1836   CIP   AC

Over the hills and far away,
One cow coughs at break of day.

Two mules moan,

Three sheep shake,

Four hens hold their heads which ache.

Five goats faint,

Six ducks doze,

Seven hogs hobble on swollen toes.

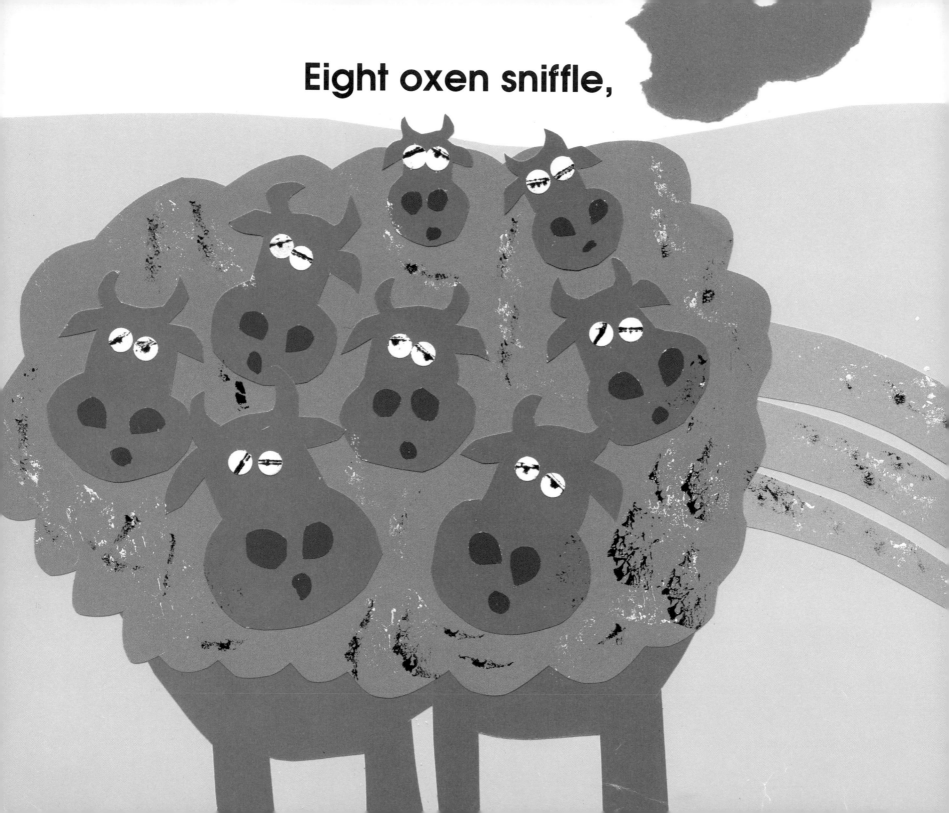

Eight oxen sniffle,

Nine geese sneeze,

Ten turkeys weep at the welts on their knees.

Far away and over the hills,
Ten turkeys swab sore knees with their quills.

Nine geese spray,

Eight oxen blow,

Seven hogs ice each delicate toe.

Six ducks gargle,

Five goats sip,

Four hens make the channels flip.

Three sheep sleep,

Two mules drink,

One cow swallows something pink.

Over the hills and far away,
Everyone feels better today.